SPIRITS N' CHAI.
Copyright @ 2022 by D. Allyson Howlett.

ISBN 979-8-9852810-3-3

Cover Design by Brittany Evans

Edited by Represent Publishing

Spirits n Chai

Spirits n Chai

D. ALLYSON HOWLETT

Represent Publishing

For Kelly. I know you'll find your Krish.

One

HE WAS OUT THERE, faded under the streetlight like someone took an eraser to him. All you could make out were the lines of what he once was. Colorless and begging to be seen. A week had gone by since he first appeared on the sidewalk across from my apartment. An entire week and no one noticed him. Except me.

It was a quarter to five, and the sun had already disappeared beneath the bay of this bustling seacoast town. Pushing what's left of my short turquoise hair behind my ear, I chewed at my lip ring as less and less people remained to challenge the cold of the streets.

Tonight was the night. I would go down there and talk to him. Once and for all.

The first day he appeared, I thought nothing of it. It was Sunday, and he was leaning against the green lamp post with his faded dark hair and dull-looking blazer and slacks. It wasn't until I ate some scrambled eggs and had a cup of tea that I noticed how transparent he looked.

As the hours rolled on, he waved his hands while people passed, saying "hello" so loudly I could hear him from my apartment window on the second floor of the gold shop. No one stopped. Not one person. Around 1:00 p.m., he seemed to have given up, and just sat defeated on the curb.

The next day, I headed out for work at the art gallery. It was around noon, and I had my dark fir rimmed pleather coat on with a homemade knit cap to keep the cold out. This was Portsmouth after all, and winters here along the Maine and New Hampshire border were always chilly.

As my dark boots hit the pavement, I spotted him staring vacantly into the street. He must have noticed me looking at him, because his eyes widened as I crossed his path. I immediately looked away, burying my face in the collar of my coat. No amount of arm flailing and shouting could bring my attention to him. I grasped onto the strap of my sloth messenger bag and kept walking as fast as I could.

He didn't stop until I turned the corner and fell against the building, my heart beating one hundred miles an hour and my nerves shot. As much as I wanted to run, I made myself peek around the corner. His features were clearer, but still barely visible. As disheveled as he was, his close shaven beard and slicked back hair appeared well kept. He was Indian, that was clear by his prominent jaw and narrow bridge. But his eyes were dark and down turned, plagued by baseball-sized circles.

On the fourth day, I couldn't take it anymore. Every night, he cried or sang a melancholy song in a language I could only guess was Hindu. Despite my bed being on the opposite side of the window that faced the street, his voice carried like black smoke seeping into the brick of the downtown shops.

I called the police and must have sounded like a crazy person. Or, at least, scared shitless by how shaky my voice was from over-rattled nerves.

When the flashing lights breached my window, I scurried over like a mouse and peeked my nose over the sill. The cop slid out of her car, holding a flashlight by her face. When the light passed over the man, it bounced off of his gray-coated frame, like fog on a rain stained road. I clasped my hand over my mouth as the cop continued looking for someone she would never find.

He was a ghost. An unseen spirit to everyone. Everyone but me.

I spent a day or two trying to decide if this man was a figment of my imagination or if he was actually there. But no amount of contemplation, and Googling every chance I got, could stifle my manic mind.

I barely slept all week. Eating was only a means of survival at this point. If I didn't go down there, I'd probably die from exhaustion or a strained heart from all the anxiety I've been dealing with.

Twisting my mouth into a knot, I grabbed my heaviest knit sweater and faux-fur boots. Before heading out the door, I wrapped my pink leopard print scarf around my neck.

Every step down the stairs was agony. My heart beat so loud, I could feel my pulse bulging out of my neck. I couldn't even grip the banister; my hands were shaking so much. No air would pass or escape my lungs.

When I reached the door to the street, I stopped to peer out the tall square window. Light snowflakes passed the pane like seeds in the silent wind. The man sat on the curb, his head hanging between his legs. Even through the streak cleaned glass, I could see the flakes pass right through him, settling on the ground on which he sat.

My hand gripped the doorknob as I finally let myself breathe. *Get it together. You can do this.* I pushed against the door and the man's face shot to focus. Dark eyes watched my petrified form as I somehow crossed the street with sheer unbridled determination.

"YOU CAN SEE ME?" The man's eyes were frantic, hands cast in front of him, anticipating my answer. His Indian accent came through and it immediately reminded me of my freshmen year philosophy professor. I'm sure he would have a field day with this.

I pulled my hands inside my sleeves, yanking at the stitching to feel its softness. The combination of tingling nerves and the crisp night air sent my bones rattling beneath my skin. Looking right at him, I could see the blue painted mailbox on the corner of the next street. His body was completely transparent, with only a slim veil of gray to show he was even there at all.

"Can you see me? Please tell me you can!" The man ran his fingers through his hair. "No. No. I know you can. I could sense it the first time you left your apartment."

The believability of this entire situation kept my mind in a fog. I couldn't tell if I was dreaming or awake. I wanted to run. As fast as my knock-off faux boots would take me.

Shutting my blue-gray eyes, I rolled my tongue over my chapped lips, landing on the metal of my lip ring. My arm muscles tightened against my body before I allowed myself to exhale a warm, nerve ridden breath. "Yes," I shuddered. "I can see you."

Opening my eyes, the man's face brightened with sudden relief. The corner of his mouth turned up into a smile and his once drooping eyes seemed to jump into his dark, full eyebrows.

"Oh, thank god. Thank god. I ... I don't know how I got here. Or why this is happening. I was ... I was in a car, and then ... I was here."

He didn't know he was dead.

I didn't know if I was numb from the cold or from the shock damaging everything I had ever known about reality. But nothing would register except the fact that this man was dead, and I was talking to him. Me. Someone who, up until recently, didn't know what it felt like to be seen at all.

The weight of being the one to tell him twisted my stomach like a wrung towel. Shifting my feet from left to right to help combat the chill, I looked down at the faint snow-covered sidewalk.

"You're ... you're dead," I whisper loud enough to carry over.

"I'm what?" His voice was stern, like I was a child telling him I flushed his watch down the toilet.

Forcing myself to look at him, I let out a scattered breath. "You're a ghost. Or maybe you're not. Maybe I'm imagining this whole thing."

Every so often, the wisps at the horizon of his see-through form fluttered in the motionless wind. Though he was still, his eyes darted in every direction. I didn't have the capacity to interpret his state of mind. Being told you were dead had to have some sort of impact on your mental health. But he had no body. He was conscious energy, or my subconscious finally coping with the trauma I had avoided dealing with for the past nine months.

"Dead?" he muttered. "No. No. No. No. No. I ... I can't be ... dead." His ghostly chest visibly heaved as his hands shook. His gray hue swelled, creating a dark cloud of uncertainty around his ghostly form. As he pushed his hands to his head, the color thickened, crawling like a shadow through the air.

All I could hear were my veins keeping time in my ears. I didn't think it was possible to be so scared and confused at the same time. Taking a step back, I shied away from whatever dark matter he was omitting. The air grew thick with what I could only describe as humidity. It pressed against my lungs and weighed me down, making it harder to move. I needed to get out of there. The longer I stood beneath the streetlamp, the more my internal organs were beginning to fail. Turning around, I made for the door leading up to my apartment.

"No, no! Please don't go!" In an instant, all evidence of despair was sucked from the street, returning it to its still state of winter crispness. The ghost flowed around me like a feather, standing before me, creating a haze between me and my escape.

"*Please*. You can't leave me here." He begged through the worry-filled wrinkles on his forehead and diamond shaped eyes.

The strings of my heart tightened from fear or sadness or both. My awkward introverted tendencies tickled my toes inside my boots, encouraging me to beat it. But I couldn't. This had to be real. Terrifying and sad all at once. I couldn't run away. I could see him. No one else had stepped forward. I did. *Why did I?*

His swirling aura beckoned me with eerie anticipation. I swallowed the next gulp of air, drying my throat to Sahara Desert levels. "What's your name?" I asked, forcing my lips and tongue to cooperate.

"I'm Krish." His gaze wandered, as if trying to remember. "Yes. My name . . . my name is Krish."

"Krish. Okay." I rubbed my hands together. "It's getting late. I need to . . . wrap my head around this. I'll . . . come back tomorrow." Crossing my arms over my chest, I puffed another heat filled cloud in his direction. It dissipated against his face, almost becoming part of him. I bit through the steady fear to not seem desperate to get away. "Is that okay?"

Krish nodded. "Yes. Yes, that's fine."

"Okay." I glanced back to the lamppost. "Try to get some rest . . . or . . . just relax, I guess." I came back to him. "I'll see you in the morning."

"Yes. Okay." He clutched his arm, rubbing up and down the sleeves of his blazer. "I'm sorry. I didn't mean to—"

"It's okay. Don't . . . don't worry about it." I tried to ignore the numbing cold he unintentionally injected into me by just being there. "My name is Raina, by the way."

"It's a pleasure to meet you." Krish mustered a smile before slowly making his way back to the lamppost. "Have a good night, Raina."

"Good night." I watched him move without making any indentations in the thin layer of snow on the ground. He settled on the curb, wrapping his arms around his legs to rest his chin on his knees. I couldn't imagine what he was thinking right now. Whatever it was, he was damn good at keeping a straight face.

Making a B-Line for my apartment door, I turned the knob to open it. But before I could pass over the threshold, I glanced back one last time. Krish's eyes caught mine, and he managed a simple wave, his face calm and filled with quiet deliberation.

I pushed against the door and fell into the stairway, shutting it behind me as quietly as I could. Leaning against the entrance, I let the tension escape through my lips in a long, drawn-out breath.

This was crazy. So much so that I couldn't be sure if I believed it. The tingling in my arm began to settle. I grasped my forearm, the slow dissipation absorbing into the soft warmth of my sweater. If this is all in my head, then I ought to win an award for having the most imaginative, whacked out mind in the world. That or be dragged away in a straight jacket.

I DIDN'T HAVE to leave until noon. Looking out my window, Krish stood amongst the bustle of downtown Portsmouth. He swayed back and forth on his heels, hands coming together in a clap before swinging them behind his back. He seemed eager. Eager and unsure.

The rock in my stomach dragged down my appetite. I wasn't ready to engage in a conversation with a ghost in broad daylight. How would I pull this off without someone thinking I was nuts?

I looked at my vintage black cat clock, its eyes shifting from left to right. 11:15 a.m. It took me twenty minutes to walk to the gallery. It was too early to leave, but the more I waited, the more I felt like jumping out the window.

Grabbing my polka dotted water bottle and messenger bag, I threw my coat and boots on and made my way to the stairs. I pulled a small clump of blue hair away from my face, clipping it back against my skull. My chopstick earrings still adorned my lobes from the other day. Usually I changed my jewelry daily, but a ghost was a pretty good excuse for breaking routine.

Krish zoomed across the street as soon as I opened the door.

Clasping his hands together, he forced a smile and bowed. "Good afternoon, Raina. So good to see you."

I stood next to him, fishing out my phone and earbuds from the front pocket of my bag. Fitting my buds into my ears, I pretended to shuffle across my phone screen. It was the only way I could survive this.

"What are you—"

"I have to go to work," I whispered, glancing at him. "You'll walk with me."

Krish nodded, though uncertainty plagued his face. "I will try."

"Try?"

"I do not know if I can leave this street. I haven't been able to."

I look around wearily. No one noticed me, which was nothing new but according to plan, at least today. "You crossed the street just now. Maybe you can come with me."

I didn't wait for a response. With a quick step to the right, I made my way down Chambers Street. Keeping my hands in the wells of my jacket pockets, I glanced down the side street before crossing onto the opposite sidewalk.

It didn't take long for Krish to fall in beside me, moving with a smoothness that only smoke could mimic. He did his best to avoid running into anyone who passed us. A few bodies made it through, but none stopped to contemplate or even notice. If they did know, I wonder what their reaction would be.

It wasn't too cold today, but cold enough that every quick huff of breath plumed in front of me. My heart beat steadily. It wasn't as desperate as the night before, but harsh enough that I could feel every beat strike against my ribcage.

"Where do you work?" Krish asked as we waited at the next corner to cross.

"The art gallery on Ceres." I glanced at him, not wanting to make complete eye contact but not wanting to be a jerk, either.

"I do not think I know it."

The light flashed from the walking man sign, showing it was time to cross. "What do you know?"

Krish sighed, drawing his attention to the ground. I kept my gaze downward, watching his feet walk in tandem with mine. Only I was creating footprints, and he wasn't.

"I remember being in a car. I believe I was driving. I cannot really recall."

Last night, the news of his fate seemed to escalate his new ghostly form. Now, he seemed to have more control. There was still a sense of chaos about him, like a dull ringing not even my ear buds could cancel out. But his color was an ambient gray, with no hints that he would expand into whatever dark form the dead could possess in times of turmoil.

"Do you remember anything before that?" I brushed past a heavily bundled man as we crossed the street again, avoiding a few stopped cars to allow more foot traffic to pass.

Krish caressed his lightly bearded chin, squeezing the impressions of his skin and pulling them downward as his brow furrowed. "It's just a shadow. Like the remnants of a memory. There was a wedding . . . yes. A wedding!" His eyes flashed, illuminating the gray of his spirit. "I was attending a wedding. My family was there. It was for . . . a sibling. I believe? I remember ... a sister and her husband, carried into a grand hall. But there's something else." His expression shifted downward as uncertainty plagued his eyes. "Something I'm missing."

My eyes watched his deep contemplation. Recounting his last days before his death, it was as debilitating as going to an actual funeral. He didn't seem too bothered by it. Probably because he couldn't remember. How can you miss something you can't remember?

As we moved onto Market Street, Krish caught me looking at him. Breaking his stagnant concentration, he formed a weak smile. "This must be strange for you."

"Strange? No. Not at all," I muttered. "I talk to ghosts all the time."

"You do?"

My head shook. "No. I was being sarcastic. Sorry. Probably not appropriate, considering the circumstances." My feet came to an unexpected halt. Clenching my eyes shut, I reluctantly turn toward my ghostly companion. "I'm sorry."

"Sorry for what?"

I forced myself to look at him. "Sorry that you died."

Floating in stillness, a few pedestrians traveled straight through him, bending his body in the direction of their stride, but not enough to disturb his gaze. "I'm sorry too."

Curiosity engulfed my mind, but I quickly forced it into submission. There are so many questions I want to ask. All rude and not empathetic. My fingers played with my hair, relentlessly tucking it behind my ear as my eyes shifted from side to side while I deliberated my words.

"You're nervous," Krish spoke calmly.

"Aren't you?"

"I . . . " his voice trailed off, his head dropping to his chest. "I'm not sure what I am." His hands rubbed up his chest, wrinkling the flaps of his blazer. "Everything I feel is new. Like discovering a new sense. Like . . . " His eyes rose to mine.

That statement sent an unnatural fear into my heart, kicking my adrenaline into high gear. Ghosts may be defined as an energy blueprint of their former selves, but this far overshadows that by a dozen or so nautical miles. I wasn't someone who freaked out about the supernatural. I used to love it as a kid. Breaking into abandoned nut houses, holding seances in cemeteries and dark basements with my friends. You know, normal odd girl stuff.

But this wasn't child's play. This was real. Real ghosts, actual death, real shit.

We continued along Market Street in silence. Questions cycled through my head like social media scrolling. Ceres came into view. The cobble-stoned street fell along the Piscataqua River, stretching out into the ocean with breathtaking clarity. Boat docks lined the riverbank, the vessels bobbing in the winter water just before the bridge. Krish slowed his stride, taking a moment to stop and admire the scenery. I waited with him, looking out across the border into Maine, watching the whisky clouds speckle the blended red and blue sky.

"Colors are . . . strange things," Krish spoke softly.

I came beside him, adjusting the straps of my bag across my shoulder. "What do you mean?"

"They're alive. Like a pulse. Surrounding everything that breathes."

My teeth clenched as a chill dripped down my spine. "That is unreasonably creepy."

"Yours is blue." His words forced my eyes upon him. With a steady hand, he searched around my circumference like he was measuring something. Carefully, he reached over my head, hovering and wiggling his fingers in the air above. "It's warm. Moving swiftly like a river."

I watched as each of his digits traveled through the empty space. The motion tickled my skin, standing my arm hair to full attention. Every passing second expedited the strangeness building up in my stomach. It tensed my muscles and shortened each sea-salted breath as it entered my lungs.

Meeting my unblinking gaze, a smirk spread across his lips. "It matches your hair."

"Okay." I took a step back, shaking the tension out through my arms. "That was . . . I don't know what that was."

"I'm sorry." He relinquished his hand. "I didn't mean to frighten you."

"No, don't apologize." My hands squeeze my arms to regain the feeling. "It's new. It's just new." I wiped my hands on my jacket and tried to seem unfazed. But I'm sure that's not possible at this point.

"I . . . I don't know what to make of this." Krish returned to search the lapping waves of the sea. "Why do I remain? If I am dead, why haven't I found the light?"

My heart sank into my stomach. "I don't know. I . . . don't know why this is happening to you. Or me. To both of us."

He looked back at me, matching my pathetic gaze with his own debilitating disbelief. "Perhaps we must find the answer. Together."

A nervous laugh erupted from my lips. "This is wild."

"I agree." He joined in my uncertain chuckle before settling down in quiet contemplation. "Will you help me?"

My tongue tangled in my throat. I wasn't the type of person to go headfirst into uncharted territory. But I had little choice in the matter. I mean, if the roles were reversed, wouldn't I want someone to help me?

"I'll try." My honesty leaking through my teeth. "That is, I'm doubtful I'll be much help. But I'll do my best."

Krish gave a simple nod, the helplessness slowly leaking from his face. I barely knew anything about this man, but I hoped I wouldn't disappoint him.

We press on, turning onto Ceres. There weren't as many people down this road, since the open sea made the air colder than if we were combing the main streets of downtown. We only managed to travel a few feet before Krish stopped in front of one of the many cafes that littered this seaside town. I watched him vividly study the building as if reliving a memory.

"Have you been here before?" I asked.

"No. I have never been here before. But," he took a hesitant step forward. "Something is here."

I looked toward the wood sided building. It was a quaint little coffee shop, adorably named *Beans n' Cream*; with a painted green and black sign hanging over the double door entrance. A few round iron tables and matching chairs sat in front, each adorned by a large pale umbrella to stifle the sun. A small fence kept the tables belonging to the establishment.

"Can we go in?" Krish looked at me with unbridled hope.

Shifting my gaze, I stared into the long paneled windows of the cafe. The coffee equipment was shining, with a bronze newness, from behind the long stretch of counter facing the sea. A large chalkboard menu covered the wall beyond the register.

I gulped down whatever moisture still clung to the inside of my mouth. "I need to get to work."

"Tomorrow then?"

I looked toward my ghostly friend, biting the inside of my lip. If I pushed myself any more today, I'm convinced my arms and legs would detach from my body. There was still a lot to process, and I wasn't sure what it all was supposed to mean. Nor did I think I ever would.

Tensing every muscle in my body, I reluctantly nodded my head. "Sure. Tomorrow."

"Thank you." He clasped his hands together. "This is difficult for you. I understand. I appreciate it."

I couldn't believe a ghost was pitying me. Me. I should pity him. He's dead. I'm not. Which is worse? An awkward 24-year-old forced to come out of her shell or a ghost whose only hope of finding closure was that said 24-year-old?

Why a more competent person wasn't chosen to help this lost soul was clearly beyond even supernatural understanding.

"Don't thank me just yet."

"I do not wish to inconvenience you. I—"

"Believe me." I turned on my heels and continued down the street. "This goes beyond inconveniencing anyone. This is so . . . unimaginably out there. I don't think normal rules apply."

A relieved laugh escaped Krish. "Yes. I suppose they don't."

YESTERDAY WENT PRETTY WELL, considering the circumstances. Krish really enjoyed the art gallery. He spent my entire shift reading up on the artists we had featured this month, giving their work a critical eye. Judging by his interest, he surely was a man of sophistication and culture. On the way home, he talked about what he had learned, asking me questions about past exhibitions and what events we held at the gallery.

I had never met anyone quite so interested in art, aside from those who thought they were better than everyone else. Art was something that shunned me for most of my teen and young adult life. Instead of swooning over boys and playing sports, I was the one sitting in the corner under the bleachers with my sketchbook. Combing over coffee table books at the bookstore. And writing papers about 15th century architecture.

It wasn't until two years ago that I met someone who seemed to mimic my life in every way possible. He fit in so well in the beginning; he was perfect. Until he peeled away the layers of my life, one small strand at a time.

"Do you have an education in art?" Krish asked on our silent walk home.

Shaking my head, I buried my nose into the fuzzy collar of my jacket to stifle the cold. "Sort of. I was going to school for studio arts, but money dried up for my dad. I had to drop out."

"There are ways you can still pursue an education."

"Drowning in debt doesn't sound that appealing."

He smiled, sliding his hands into his coat pockets. "Well, the gallery gives you a window. How long have you been working there?"

"About a year. I run shows sometimes."

"Ah." Krish leaned closer to me, breaking my personal space bubble. "There are more galleries in the world you can aspire to be a part of. Other than this one."

I shook my head. "I'm not a very ambitious person."

But the more we walked, the more I thought about how cool it would be to run an art gallery in Boston or New York. *Me? A curator at a New York City art gallery?* As the thought crept into my brain, my stomach turned on itself. I could never do that, not me. I wasn't meant to do anything like that. I was just something to admire for a little while. Not meant to have an option, let alone make an impact. At least, that was the old me. But I didn't know who this new me was either. I was caught in the middle. In the middle of me.

"What is wrong?" Krish's genuine concern melted away the memories of my past.

Raising my shoulders, I forced a smile. "What makes you think something's wrong?"

He hesitated, sliding his hands into his blazer. "Your aura. It's changing."

Perfect. There would be no hiding my feelings from him, it seemed. "Guess I can't hide anything from you." A nervous smile breached my lips. "Maybe I'm not supposed to."

"You do not need to tell me if it is too personal."

"No, I—" A rock jumped into my throat to shut me up. Even

after nine months, it felt wrong to talk about it. Like I was breaking the rules. Rules I no longer abided by since leaving him, but still felt tethered to. "I was in a pretty controlling relationship for a while. I wasn't allowed to be myself or . . . anything. At all." I looked away from him to try and keep the boulder from escaping. "It was . . . very hard to leave."

"But you did."

He spoke so confidently; I was able to look at him without feeling like I did something wrong. My initial reaction to interacting with a ghost was fear-based, but now that I've spent the day with him, it was strangely gratifying. Refreshing almost. Krish was a spirit of confidence, despite the moments of credited confusion and uncertainty. He was remarkably easy to talk to. Because he was dead? Maybe. Or because he didn't have a choice but to listen to my agonizing past. One I wished I could erase for all eternity.

"WHAT'S WITH THE BLUE HAIR?"

My entire body tensed hearing Paul's condescending tone. Standing in the kitchen, I put a glass, freshly washed, into the drying rack. I didn't bother to turn around as he approached me. His looming presence casting a shadow over my so-called life. Shoving the nauseous feeling deep down into my gut, I continued to wash the dishes, grabbing another glass as the water flowed over its surface.

"I wanted a change, that's all."

"Is that the new thing now?" He dragged his fingers along the edges of my hair, sending chills down my spine. "You and your trends."

He walked toward the fridge, releasing his hold on me enough so I could breathe without it hurting. "I'll entertain it for now. But you should dye it back before the week is over."

My mind wretched with total disgust. "Why?"

I heard the fridge open, the sounds of shifting Tupperware and bottles shot through me like sharp stones pelting my skin. "We can't go to my parents' house this Saturday with you looking like that. What will my family think of you, seeing you deface yourself like this? A beautiful girl like you shouldn't ruin her looks just because it's popular. I can't have you pretending to be something you're not, not when I'm trying to keep up appearances with my folks."

The sponge dropped from my hand into the sink. I held on to the glass under the faucet, staring at the etching of my name and his along its surface. This was the gift he gave me for our one-year anniversary, marking the day everything about our relationship changed.

Shutting my eyes, I held my lips taut, biting into the soft tissue on the inside of my mouth. The points of my fingers felt hot beneath the running water as the nausea clawed its way up my esophagus. The next words I wanted to say hung at the back of my throat like bird shit on a window. But I had to scrape it off. I couldn't stand the feeling of it lingering on the edge.

"I'm not changing it."

The fridge door shut, and I heard Paul's sneakers pivoting on the linoleum floor. "What did you say?"

My eyes shot open as I turned to face his smug expression. "I'm not changing my hair."

He smirked, tilting his head as his smooth stride carefully approached me. The glass still clenched in my hand; I don't think I blinked once as he came to stand in front of me. "If you don't change it, I'll cut it off while you sleep."

I couldn't move. Let alone breath. His long spider-legged fingers came up to my face. An arrogant chuckle rumbled from his partially closed lips. "Come on, Raina. I'm only kidding. You know I wouldn't cut off your hair." He tucked my hair behind my multi-pierced ear. "We'll go to the convenience store later and pick out a nice color for you. I'll help you dye it."

He brought his smug expression close to mine, his stale breath seeping into my nostrils. "Don't you want me to find you attractive?"

In the blink of an eye, I smashed the glass against his jaw, shat-

tering it into a million pieces across the floor. Paul clutched his face, reeling as he stepped back from the shards left embedded in his flesh.

"YOU FUCKING BITCH!" Blood dripped from the spaces between his fingers, pooling onto the floor in time with the rushing water still escaping from the faucet.

I turned around, grabbed my bag off the hook, and shot through the door. Running down the stairs, tears poured from my eyes as I heard him yelling down the corridor after me. My heart was in a race with itself, begging my feet to move faster. I didn't stop. I ran. As far and as fast as I could. I ran and never looked back.

I WOKE up in a dry sweat. Air couldn't cycle through my lungs fast enough. Looking out my window, the sun had already risen, meaning it was at least 8:00 a.m. I pulled my crocheted blanket over my knees and wrapped my arms around them. It's been a long time since I dreamed about Paul or anything related to the life I escaped from. I guess talking to Krish about it, no matter how subtle it was, rattled those memories from the grave.

It was a new day. A day without Paul suffocating me into oblivion. I had to be grateful for that. Despite being nine months since I left, I still didn't feel whole. Maybe he took more from me than I thought. If I would ever get it back, who knew. I was pretty content to be this way forever.

I ripped the blankets from my bed and hopped onto the floor. It was time to get moving, away from the bad memories. Nothing beat those away like the notion I had a ghost to host, in a manner of speaking. A ghost who was stuck here until he found whatever he needed to find.

After taking a quick shower and grabbing a bite from my tiny kitchen, I bundled up and shot out the door to join Krish at the corner. He had a welcoming smile as I crossed the street to meet him, throwing my hair into some messy bun pigtails. The second I came beside him, his smile diminished.

"What's wrong?" he asked with an almost melted expression.

"Nothing." I shrugged. "I ... had a bad dream, is all."

"Dreams are usually a window to something bigger. Do you want to talk about it?"

"Not particularly." We waited together on the corner, letting the light snow pass, or in his case, through. "Come on. Let's get to your cafe."

CAFE FOLK usually kept to themselves. It wasn't the people I was uncomfortable with, but the *amount* of people. Especially in the morning.

Rubbing the sweat from my hands across my black spotted leggings, I shivered in my boots as we approached the door. Raising my hand to grip the handle felt like moving a monster truck tire, but luckily, someone was coming out and graciously held the door for me.

So far, so good.

I smiled as we entered the cafe, absorbing the warm atmosphere of this friendly, caffeine-ridden establishment.

Krish stood right behind me, waiting to advance to the counter. But my feet were glued to the floor. I did experience lapses of nerves in unfamiliar places, but this was different. Maybe because I had an agenda, a reason for being here that was so out of this world, I barely believed it.

"Raina?" Krish's questioning voice coiled in my ear. "Are you going to order something?"

I almost blurted out a response, but held my tongue. A girl talking to herself in the middle of a cafe was not the attention I wanted. Scurrying up to the counter, a glasses-wearing brunette stood ready to greet me. She was wearing a red and gray camo print shirt and tight pre-ripped jeans.

"Hi," she said with a bubbly smile. "What can I get for you today?"

Fiddling with my purple painted nails, I looked up at the chalkboard menu. At my current level of uneasiness, everything looked jumbled and turned upside down. I tried my best to focus, but it was becoming impossible with the added pressure to perform.

The brunette seemed to notice my indifference as she leaned against the counter to peer at the board. "Any flavors you're into?"

Twisting my mouth, I glanced at her. "I'm not much of a coffee drinker."

"We have some great teas. Our signature vanilla chai is our most popular."

"Sure, let's go with that."

She smiled and typed in my order. "What size?"

"Small is fine."

I gave her my cat face debit card, which she took courteously. "Cute card." After a few seconds and a signature later, she handed my card back. "Can I have a name?"

I hesitated, like my name was too sacred to utter aloud. "Raina."

"It'll be right out for you, Raina." I tucked my card back into the slot behind my phone. "By the way," the girl's continued conversation startled me, "love your hair."

A half-smile crept upon my face. "Thanks."

I slipped from the counter and walked to the bar along the window. Finding the farthest stool from civilization, I popped down and immediately pulled out my phone to avoid any further social interactions. Though the barista's comment stuck in my head, lifting my spirits a bit. She liked my hair. And no one chose it but me.

The entire time I was at the counter, I had completely forgotten about Krish. When he slid onto the stool next to me, I jumped in my seat. Krish didn't seem to notice; not even a blink could break his concentrated stare.

"What's up?" I whispered as I trolled through my phone.

"That man there." He pointed a steady finger. "There is something . . . familiar about him."

Curiosity overtook my need to hide. I followed his gaze to a guy sitting at one of the small round tables, his left side facing us. He had dark, curly hair sitting in a neat mop against shaved sides. A black knit jacket covered his tight arms as he sat hunched over a wafting beverage. My observation traveled down to his legs, which were bouncing nervously in acid-washed jeans and slick ankle-high boots. A few rings glistened against his left hand, complimenting his sand-coated complexion.

It was like Aladdin jumped out of the Disney movie and raided a Neiman Marcus.

With a slight brow raise, Aladdin turned and caught my dull blue eyes. For a second, I admired how deep his eyes were. But only for a second.

"Vanilla Chai for Raina!"

I sprang from my seat, pulling my scarf over my mouth as I approached the counter. Grabbing my tea, I practically ran back to my seat to avoid any chances of me looking at Krish's newfound interest.

Hunkering down, I pushed my drink forward, resting my chin on my arms. Not even gritting my teeth could calm the seething embarrassment dancing in my stomach right now.

"He's looking at you." Krish didn't seem to notice my blatant bashfulness.

"Thank you." I buried my face in my arms. "Did not need to know that."

"Can you go over to him?"

My head shook on autopilot. "No way. No freaking way."

"You must . . . I mean." Krish lowered his head to my level. "His aura, or energy . . . It is what I felt yesterday."

"Well, have you seen him before?" I asked without allowing my face to breach the texture of my jacket.

"No. Never. But . . . he is the source." His attention shifted back to the man in question. "I'm sure of it."

I ventured another peek at the so-called chosen one. He wasn't looking our way anymore, just mildly sipping on his drink with an elbow on the table. Even though his leg was still bouncing, it was the only part that looked remotely movable. Tension oozed from his tight posture, clearly trying to keep something from spilling out.

"He looks uneasy." I rose from my hiding place. "I can't just walk up to him. What would I even say?" I took a nervous sip of my chai, which sat appealingly in a large tan-coated mug of frothy goodness. Nutmeg and cinnamon spice floated on the top. The minute it hit my tongue, its rich taste settled the gremlins that ran rampant in my stomach.

Krish retreated against his chair, causing the wisps of his ghostly form to waft at the edges. "Will you try? Please."

A dragging sigh deflated the awkwardness into my warm, steaming belly. The chai really did the trick in calming my unbridled nerves. Maybe I could do this. Or maybe I'd crash and burn on contact.

Krish put his hand on the bar, leaning forward. "If you do and it's nothing, we leave. You never have to return here again. There is nothing to lose."

"Only my dignity," I mumbled under my breath.

That got a chuckle out of him. "You are always this dramatic?"

I stifled a faint laugh at my absurdity. "No. Usually not."

He eyed Aladdin again, drawing my gaze to the restless Arabian knight. "I do not wish to make you uncomfortable. But I must know. What this could possibly mean."

I took a deep breath, swallowing any gremlins down that were still trying to overtake me. He was right. We were a team. Haphazardly thrown together, but a team nonetheless. If we ever wanted to figure out what this meant, I couldn't let anything hold me back.

I grabbed my mug of chai and took a nice, satisfying gulp. "All right." I returned the mug to the table with a thud. "Let's do this."

Pushing off my stool, I straightened my jacket and turned toward my target.

"Raina, you've got—"

I didn't wait for Krish to finish, as my feet moved in a straight line toward Aladdin's table. My heartbeat echoed with every heel-to-floor stride, rippling the aftershock through my entire body.

Saying "hi" to a guy—an attractive guy at that—was absolutely terrifying. Since Paul, I have never even looked at another guy. I avoided them. Any guy that looked this good was either a complete asshole or too uptight for the likes of me. Now I was forcing one such guy to at least acknowledge my existence. If I told myself two weeks ago I would be doing this, I would have laughed in my own face.

Before I could even think of second guessing myself, I'm standing in front of his table. Planting my boots firmly on the smooth imitation stone floor, I watched as his attention fell on me.

Not a sound escaped as he looked at me with his brow raised and the corner of his mouth slowly drawing upward. I attempted to clear my throat, but it came out more like a squeak.

"Um . . . excuse me?" he said, raising a few loose fingers to grace his nose. "You've got something . . . "

My body went rigid. "What?"

"Something . . . " he scratched his nose, "on your nose."

Somehow, through my tunneling vision, I wiped my hand over my face. I could feel moisture smear across my knuckles. Pulling my hand into view, I spy some chai tea froth, with a hint of nutmeg, thin against my skin.

"Shit." I don't give him a chance to respond, as I've already burst through the front door and onto the street.

The hair on the back of my neck rose, sending spider sensations into the pit of my stomach. I created as much distance between me and the coffee shop as I could.

I knew I'd blow it. *Stupid, stupid, stupid.*

Somehow, Krish is gliding beside me. "I tried to tell you."

"You could have been more forward."

"We will try again."

"No." I turned swiftly on my heels to face him. "I can't go back there now that I've embarrassed myself!"

"Perhaps you just need a day to—"

"Krish. No."

The graying lines of his form began to swirl and turn outward. "You'd give up so easily?"

"I'm not giving up. I just ... it's not easy for me to just go up to someone and talk to them like that."

"I understand."

"No. You don't. Guys are poisonous. All of them. Fucking poison and should be avoided." My eyes shut. Maybe I was being too harsh, but the gremlins were in full force now. Crawling up my shoulders and whispering doubt into my ears. This was exactly what I was afraid of. The tense, debilitating feeling started to come back. That feeling I had every waking moment of my life with Paul.

I had no clue what kind of person Krish was before he died. But he didn't seem like someone who would allow himself to be caught in a situation like that, doubted himself and his ability to function as a human being.

I could never go back there. It's tainted now. My awkward social graces hungered for embarrassment. It became number 327 in my places to never find myself again for as long as I live.

I took a deep breath and held it in my lungs for what seemed like an unfathomable amount of time. By the time I released, my eyes fell open to a swirling tornado of darkness slowly reaching into the sky from where Krish stood. He hovered at its center, fists clenched and black gaze focused. I didn't know how to be scared at this point, but the sheer rate of whatever unhinged energy this mass was producing shrunk me down to miniature proportions.

"Krish," I spoke softly. "What's happening to you?"

The moment my words breached the cloud, Krish fell backward like he was trying to keep himself steady. His hands opened and ran through his hair. A harsh exhale extinguishing the void surrounding him, like someone blowing out a candle.

"I . . . I do not know what that was." He closed his eyes, shaking his head as the gray returned.

Biding my time, I waited until there wasn't a single speck of black left contorted around him. "It happened before."

His head twisted toward me, eyes poised at my confession. "It has?"

Pressing my lips together, I tossed my lip ring back and forth to garner some sort of control over this unexplainable phenomena. I didn't want to exacerbate this any longer. I needed to be calm, for him. Maybe my self-doubt and defiance was making him turn into ... something else. I don't know if that even sounded rational.

"Let's go home," I said, walking up to him as his gaze settled on me. "Take a step back. Maybe try again another day."

"Yes," he whispered breathlessly. "Perhaps that is a good idea."

NOT TALKING about what happened only made being around Krish that much worse. Part of me was afraid I would ignite the black fire again, or whatever ghost hunters wanted to call it. Staring at him from my window, his appearance had diminished. His hair and clothes were disheveled more so than when I first saw him. The bags under his eyes seemed to deepen, making his dark eyes more intense the longer you stared into them.

Feeling like I had to justify myself to a dead guy spoke volumes. Desperation was an understatement. We were both desperate in some way. I didn't know what the situation was doing to him, in his mind or his energy cloud or whatever. But it was clear as day as he sat with his hands hanging between his knees, letting town-goers run through him like a car cutting through a puddle of water, that he was suffering.

I had the day off on Saturday. The weather called for a rocket high of 30 degrees. That's warm for January. A light snow still coated the streets, scattered atop the curb and rooftops of the local businesses.

I threw on a long sleeve black and gray tunic and some knitted leggings. Grabbing a canvas and my watercolor case, I hopped down the stairs and breached the door to the outside world. It was early, so the streets were mostly vacant.

Krish looked at me with sad eyes. Walking over to him, I waved the canvas in my sparkle-gloved hands. "Hey. I was going to head down to the shore and do some painting. Want to tag along?"

He sat against the lamppost and looked away, his once well kept hair lying in disarray. His suit was more wrinkled and stained. The top buttons of his graying shirt were missing completely.

When he didn't respond, I shifted in my stance, bending down to him. "Look. I'm sorry about what happened on Wednesday."

His head dropped even farther into his chest. "I am dead. My life is over. So what does it matter? If I am doomed to remain this way forever, then so be it."

Instinct told me to leave it alone, but I forced myself to reach out to him. With a steady hand, I aimed for his shoulder. I knew I'd pass right through him, but I couldn't think of anything else to do. Instead of watching his graying form dissipate and reappear, it landed. Krish's gaze darted to where I fell, looking into my wide-eyed expression. There was no mention of being able to do this in ghost documentaries or theories of science. My fingers wanted to retract, but I bit through the urge to flee. The surface of his tattered blazer was smooth, despite the visible damage. There was no warmth or cold coming off him. Just a gentle throbbing, like he still had a pulse.

The moment ticked by without much of a reaction. We just looked at each other, each wondering if the other had the answer. I finally drew my hand away, unable to shake the tingling nerves set off in my fingertips. "Okay . . . that was . . ."

"Raina." His ghostly hand took my wrist, pulling us both to stand. "I do not know what's happening to us. But there must be a reason. I am sorry if I have disrupted your life. But," he carefully let go, "I am grateful to you. Truly I am."

The back of my throat began to close. Whatever it was that forced Krish on me either did it for a reason or wanted to watch us squirm. I didn't ask to be haunted by a cultured gentleman. Someone I would never in a million years associate with outside of my profession. He's nowhere on my level, residing on top while I'm scratching at the floor. He had a confidence in me I didn't even have in myself. All because he had to believe I could help find the answer.

I nodded excessively to push any sadness back down. "I know. I'm grateful too. In a supernatural way."

He smiled, pushing his dark hair from his face. "Thank you, my friend."

After a few seconds, I let a stifle of nervous energy out through my teeth. "So, you coming with me?"

"Of course. I would love to."

We headed toward the shore, with the sun slowly climbing above the horizon to meet us. There were a few suitable spots for painting. Having an understanding with Krish, I was far less worried about being caught talking to myself as we made our way down the street.

Krish absorbed my ramblings like a champ. Maybe he was genuinely interested, or maybe just trying to be a good listener. Either way, it felt good. I was talking so much; I didn't realize we were cresting the corner of Market and Ceres. My body went this way so often, autopilot was getting us there.

The light crested the silent roll of the waves as they lapped against the shoreline. If you looked to the left, the iron beamed bridge echoed with a gentle hum from any early bird drivers daring to cross the frigid waters. A few boats dotted the horizon, gearing up for some cold water catches.

We stepped around to the corner, taking a few quiet seconds to admire the morning. The cold sea air tried to penetrate my warm knit jacket, but to no avail.

"Has your art been featured at the gallery?" Krish asked as he settled his hands in his pockets.

"No. The owners say they'd look at my work and consider it. But none of my paintings are good enough."

"According to who?" I glanced as he raised an eyebrow at my pessimism.

"According to my negative outlook."

"Well," he said as we continued our stroll. "How do you know if you don't try? What is the worst that can happen? They say yes, you move forward. They say no, you are right where you were before."

"I hear you, and you're right." I walked backward to face him. "Doesn't mean I'll do it."

"Hey there."

Krish stopped to look to his left. My eyes followed and fell upon the cozy little cafe I had the pleasure of embarrassing myself in just a few days before. Sitting at one of the many round iron tables scattered about the front patio was Aladdin. His hands wrapped around a steaming hot ceramic cup, tall enough to hold more than the amount of caffeine the human body should consume in a day. He looked right at me with a half-smile across his five o'clock shadow. A dark North Face aided his attempt to sit in the wintry morning air. The same ankle boots adorned his feet, complimented by a pair of black speckled jeans. A black and white scarf sat cozily around his neck.

My arms dropped to my sides, standing like a deer in the headlights. I glanced at Krish, who did nothing but wait with a patient expression. Looking down the street, my gaze came back to the cafe. "Were you talking to me?"

Aladdin's half-smile became a full one. "Who else would I be talking to?"

I remembered he couldn't see Krish, and physically, I was the only being on the street. *Of course, he's talking to me.* The realization turned up the dial on my nerves, releasing the gremlins into a proper sweep of my insides. My grip on the square canvas tightened. "Oh."

Aladdin glanced down the road along the shoreline. "Are you in a rush?"

I shook my head, wishing like hell I could lie in situations like this. "No, just . . . out for a little walk."

"Would you like to sit down?" He gestured to the empty seat across from him, welcoming my warm body to take a load off.

My muscles tightened as I chewed on my lip ring. "For what reason?"

Shifting in his seat, he glimpsed to the right before returning to me with a raised eyebrow. "Are you always this cautious?"

"When a strange person asks me to sit with him. Yeah. I better be."

A light, breath-filled chuckle escaped with a flash of his teeth. "You didn't seem to have an issue walking up to me the other day."

I didn't think I could move if I wanted to, but Krish placed a supportive hand on my lower back. Before I knew it, I was sitting across from the Arabian knight, with Krish sitting at the table beside us.

I placed my canvas and paints on the table before curling my hands back into my lap.

"Do you want anything to drink?" he asked in a polite tone.

"No. Thanks. I'm okay." I squished my hands between my legs, casting uneasy glances between Krish and the table's surface.

"I'm Ameel, by the way." He held out a gloved hand, waiting for me to do the polite thing.

I could barely pull mine from my thigh trap, but took his and offered a gesture of introduction. "Raina."

"That's a pretty name." Our hands parted as quickly as they came together. He wrapped his back around his cup. "It suits you."

"Why does it suit me?"

"Well, Raina. Rain. Your hair is blue. Is that on purpose?"

His observation both surprised and annoyed me. I never put my love for vibrant-colored hair and my name together. Not even my current mermaid shade of blue. I liked the color. And it matched, in a cheesy, childish kind of way.

Self-consciously, I moved my fingers through my hair, making sure it was still tucked behind my decorated ears. "I honestly never thought about it before."

Silence fell over the table. I rested my hands on its surface, pulling at my gloves as I tried to think of something else to say. Ameel tapped the side of his mug, tightening his mouth, unsure how to proceed. A soft draft of sea air, mixed with his Old Spice aroma, tickled my nose. I could tell he used the BearGlove fragrance, because it's the one I most awkwardly sniffed at CVS when I had to stock up on bathing products. I had a bottle in my shower, not gonna lie.

"So," he finally got out. "You're an artist?"

My head snapped back to attention. "Why would you think that?"

"The canvas and paints." He eyed my obvious art supplies sitting on the table.

"Oh." My arm shot out to grab them, slowly sliding them into my lap. "I dabble, I guess you could say. Nothing serious."

"Sounds familiar."

"What?"

Ameel ran his hand over his chin, covering his mouth before leaning back in his seat. "Sorry. It's nothing." His gaze fell to his right, accompanied by a sigh I could only guess was out of frustration or nerves.

Krish leaned his elbows on his knees and watched Ameel closely. I wished I could see what he was seeing right now. If Krish was picking up on this guy's aura, I bet it was changing colors faster than a chameleon.

My hands pressed into the empty canvas, now secured to my lap. If I put any more pressure on it, I was certain I'd destroy any chance of catching a beautiful morning in paint across its surface.

"So." Ameel adjusted his chair, crossing his arms on the table. "I haven't seen you around here the past few days. Have you been avoiding it on purpose?"

My heart jumped into my throat. He would only say that if he was expecting me to come back here. Waiting for me to resurface so he could interact with me. Had he come every day to see if I'd be here?

"After I embarrassed myself, yes. I have been."

The words coming out of my mouth shocked me to my core. I was proceeding with an escalated bitchiness. Usually I was a pretty friendly individual, but this guy. I don't know. There was something about him I couldn't read right off the cusp. He was dodging, same as I was. We were both skating around something. Mine more obvious, of course.

"I wasn't trying to embarrass you," he confessed politely. Ameel took a sip from his cappuccino filled mug, pressing his lips together to savor the bitter taste. "Why did you come up to me, anyway?"

I couldn't come out with the truth, nor could I think of a good lie. Rolling my tongue over the bottom of my gums, I shifted in my seat. "You wouldn't believe me if I told you."

Ameel popped a grin, his posture straightening in his chair. "Try me."

My eyes narrowed, and my posture tightened along my back. "I'd rather not try."

"Alright. Your walls are up. I get it." He reached behind his neck as he leaned back.

I chanced a glance at Krish, who looked on eagerly like someone watching a film, expecting something to happen. Settling back onto the table, my hair fell against my cheek. "Maybe I will take that drink after all."

"Sorry, that offer has left the building," he said rather smugly.

My brows skyrocketed upward. "Aren't you supposed to be a gentleman to a complete stranger?"

"Who said you were a stranger? I know your name. You know

mine. We're on an acquaintance level now."

"Fine." I folded my arms against my chest and huffed into the cold air, looking toward the sea. "Have it your way."

"What? No fight in the bull? You look tougher than that."

My head snapped back to him. A white-toothed grin smeared all over his dangerously charming face. If he wasn't so nice to look at, I would have left right then, but this wasn't over yet. He was hiding something. Something Krish could only see in his current state of being. But me, I could find a way to pull it out of this guy. Then maybe Krish would be free.

"Tell you what." He leaned forward. "You tell me why you came up to me a few days ago, and I'll get you anything off the menu."

He was playing hardball and enjoying himself in the process. These are the kind of jerks I usually avoided, but this was for Krish. And maybe a chance for me to flex my muscles a bit.

"All right." I glanced at Krish before settling back on Ameel. "I was going to comment on how you looked like Aladdin."

Ameel's hand came up to catch his uncomfortable laughter. "What?" I watched as he continued to find a way to hold himself together.

I kept my Van Damme card in play, leaning forward slightly. "The chai latte, if you don't mind."

Ameel took a moment to settle down, watching the intensity on my face as his expression began to cool. "Alright." Ameel pushed his chair to stand. "Be right back."

Leaving the table, he disappeared inside the cafe. I turned to Krish with unbridled nerves dripping from my fingers. Krish sat up, eager to listen to what I couldn't contain.

"Please tell me you see something." My shoulders flexed up my back as I let some nervous energy out through my teeth. "I don't know how much longer I can withstand his jerkiness."

Krish shifted his gaze, looking everywhere and nowhere at the same time. His mind was working overtime, trying to figure something out by the crease in his brow and the tight fold of his lips.

"What's wrong?"

"I don't know . . . but," he focused on me, "remember when I told you about seeing your energy? Your aura?"

Resting my elbows on my lap with a subtle nod, I waited for him to elaborate.

Krish's tongue rolled across his bottom lip before pressing them down again in deep contemplation. "It's changing. The more you sit with this man, it's becoming something else. Calmer, tranquil. Shifting from a harsh blue. Mixing with his crimson."

This sounded like something out of sci-fi movie, horror, or a combination of both. Hearing him explain what his observations of us were felt like a complete violation of privacy. But he couldn't help it. He was on a different plane of existence. And by the looks of him, as troubled by it as I was.

"Calmer? Nothing about this conversation is calm." I rubbed my eyes, still as confused as ever. "What does it mean?"

Krish shook his head, raising his hands in surrender. "I do not know. But whatever it is, it is strong. Pulling me in like a moth to a fire. I can almost feel its warmth. It's welcoming and ... quite exhilarating."

"Glad you seem to be enjoying yourself."

"I also remember something."

My reluctant state of being shifted immediately as his statement sunk in. I straightened my posture, seeing that he wasn't done revealing the clue that was unearthed from this unlikely conversation.

"One. Yes." He eased into the seat. "A ferry. Riding across the Hudson River. The Statue of Liberty in the distance. I'm . . . leaning against the railing, overlooking the water as the boat cuts through the waves. When something catches my eye. Standing at the bow . . . flowing in the forced wind like a feather gliding through the air . . ." He stopped, trailing off into the clouds of his ghostly figure.

I waited for him to continue, but he was lost. Consumed by this memory that he still can't seem to grasp on to. "Krish?"

The cafe door opened and Ameel walked out with my chai in hand. He placed it on the table, careful to avoid any chance of spilling a single drop. "Here you go, Ariel."

I swung my legs back under the table. "Ariel?" The tantalizing aroma of nutmeg and cinnamon was enough to stifle a rise in my annoyance levels.

Ameel sat back down in his chair. "Yeah. I'm Aladdin. So you're Ariel."

I wrapped my hands around my tea, taking in the comforting warmth through my fingers. "I look nothing like Ariel."

"Why? Because her hair is red and yours is blue?"

"Among other things." I brought the mug to my lips, savoring the delicious taste as it coated my mouth. If it wasn't for this beverage, my blood pressure would be through the roof with all this bickering.

"So, do all Middle Easterners look like Aladdin? Is that what you're suggesting?"

I almost choked on my tea, but managed to force it down with a hard swallow. Clearing my throat, I pressed my fist against my chest before making my recovery. "No."

He folded his arms against his chest. "Because that's what it sounds like."

I wasn't trying to be offensive. I meant it as a compliment. Aladdin was my childhood crush since I was 6 years old, but I couldn't tell him that. He definitely didn't act like Aladdin. More like the monkey, Abu. Kind of nice, but also a complete jerk when it came down to it.

"I meant it as a compliment," I spoke calmly, keeping my hands wrapped around my mug to ground myself.

"Well, don't assume someone will take it as that."

"Are you always this argumentative?"

"Are you always so inconsiderate?"

"Wow." I pushed my tea forward and stood up. "Well. Thank you for the tea." Throwing my bag over my shoulder, I gathered my art supplies. "You really know how to make a first impression."

Krish stood with me, his gaze swimming with fixed uncertainty. This guy was a complete asshole. As much as I wanted to help him, there was no way I was going to sit here and spend my morning arguing with the likes of Ameel.

Before I made it around the table, Ameel stood up. "Wait."

I stopped, eyeing him as he looked toward his right again, rubbing the back of his head with a weary hand.

"I didn't mean to come off as a jerk." His eyes caught mine. "I'm sorry."

My lip curled in the corner of my mouth as I eagerly tapped my boots on the slick concrete. "Thank you. And I apologize if I offended you. That wasn't my intention."

"Can I make it up to you?"

His request forced my eyes to widen. What was the purpose of him wanting to hang out with me? He clearly didn't find my company enjoyable and vice versa. But as he waited for my response, there was a glint of hopefulness in his eyes.

"Why?" I asked. "We clearly don't get along."

He shrugged. "We don't have to."

A defiant *NO* was dripping from my tongue. If it weren't for Krish, I'd kick this jerk to the curb and be done with him. But there was a small part of me that felt more alive bickering with this guy. I was confident. Not afraid that I'd say something wrong. I didn't notice until now, but the moment we started getting into the meat of our conversation, the gremlins in my stomach vanished. Could this all be connected somehow? God only knew at this point.

With a deep sigh, I watched Krish as he waited for my response. He didn't make any gesture or indication that he wanted me to say yes, but I knew deep down, something was pulling him to create this situation. The answers weren't found yet. We barely scratched the surface.

"Sure," I finally said. "Why not."

Seven

"SO," Ameel tapped a finger on the table, "you work at an art gallery? That's cool."

We sat inside the cafe, trying to make small talk. It was awkward, not gonna lie. Trying to pull any interest out of this conversation was minimal, at best. This second meeting, or whatever it was, was less tense than the first, at least for me. Ameel seemed cooler, but his leg was bouncing under the table again with an unsteady foot peeking out from the edge.

Krish watched us from the wall, leaning inside the corner like it would swallow him up. I had a hard time looking at him lately. His face was now gaunt, almost like he was decaying right before my eyes.

"What do you do?" I forced my question as I lightly tapped my purple nails against the mug of chai sitting in front of me.

Ameel smirked, adjusting himself in his suave leather jacket. "If I told you, I'd have to kill you."

"Ha," I almost grunted. "You're funny."

"Come on, lighten up." He leaned into the table. "You seem so tense."

"And you're not?" I peered at his neurotic foot. "Your leg hasn't stopped moving since we sat down."

"Nothing gets past you."

"What is *that* supposed to mean?"

I don't know what it was, but Ameel really knew how to push my buttons. Maybe I was being a little excessive in my defensiveness, but it was something I couldn't shut off. This is the most interaction I've had with a guy in nine months. Nine months of isolation, with nothing but my thoughts and my canvas. I had a lot of time to think in nine months, and nothing to show for it. I hadn't been able to change or better myself. Stuck in an endless loop of looking over my shoulder.

He shook his head with a pithy smile. "You don't have many friends, do you?"

My back straightened as I sat up in my seat, taken aback by his brashness. "Excuse me?"

Leaning in his chair, he shrugged against the vertical wooden seat back. "You're the most defiant person I've ever met."

My hand came away from the mug and balled into a fist beside it. "You don't know anything about me."

"I doubt anyone does. The rate you chew people up."

"What is your problem?"

He came up off the seat back. "My problem is having to sit through this conversation."

The pulse behind my eyes blurred my vision. I glanced at Krish, who only stared at us with an almost vacant expression. How much longer did I have to endure this test? Ameel clearly was a complete jerk, and yet, I was forced to sit through his antagonistic attitude and try to get something concrete from this. The thing that Krish so-called saw in him. One more minute and I was ready to walk.

"You invited me." My voice was stern. "I told you not to bother."

"But you came anyway. Why? To act like a little shit . . . " His face dropped, shrinking back like a scolded child. "I'm sorry. I'm . . . not usually like this."

My fingers relaxed around my mug, ready to throw my guard back up at any moment. "Like what? A complete asshole?"

With a slight nod, Ameel's chin sank deeper into the shadow of himself. "I am an asshole."

The silence that passed between us gave me a chance to come down. I waited for him to recover from whatever emotional crisis he was facing within himself. To get that hair raised with a complete stranger . . . we were both protecting ourselves from the other. I wasn't someone who aired out my dirty laundry to just anyone. Especially a guy like him. The more we sat there, I'd come to realize how little people knew about what happened between me and Paul. My brother did, but he just got angry. He didn't listen. And Krish ... but I barely let him peek at the entire Andy Warhol chaos my life had been. What it still was.

"Hey." Ameel slowly looked at me, his face sullen in uncomfortable uncertainty. "Can I tell you something?"

I swallowed hard, preparing myself for some deplorable nonsense. But his eyes were shifting with fear, like this wasn't a joke anymore. Laying my hands flat against the table, I gave myself another moment to deflate. "Sure."

He straightened his posture, looking dead out into the open cafe before bringing his hands together in front of him.

"I dated . . . this girl for a while." He came back for a glance at my patient gray-blue eyes. "Years, actually. We were a couple, not just dating." His shoulders tensed for a second and then came back down again. "She told me she wanted to take the next step in our relationship. Marriage. Kids. Full commitment for the rest of our lives."

Looking down at his hands seemed to save him from his confession for a moment. But the hesitation didn't last much longer. "She was ready for it. But ... I wasn't. I don't know what it was, but ... I was scared to tell her the truth. That I wasted her time all those years we were together. How scared I was to take that step, even with her. I don't know. So I ... fucked it up."

"How?" His gaze rose at my single word. The gremlins were at work again, but it felt different this time. I didn't feel anxious, nervous maybe. Whatever he was about to tell me would bring some sense to all this, somehow. I'd forgotten that people were people, no matter where they came from. Bad things happened to everyone. All of them. I wasn't the only one. I wasn't alone.

Ameel pressed his lips together in hesitation. "I pushed her away. Treated her like shit. I . . . I cheated on her." A nerve-rattled breath shook his gaze to his still-folded hands. "I cheated on her so many times."

His hand came across his forehead, disrupting the smoothness of his skin with lines and crevasses of his own making. They folded his brows together, coming back down to land helplessly on the table's surface.

"When she found out, I didn't even bat an eye. Didn't deny it. She left with my ridicule in her ear and tears polluting her face. And I didn't even try to stop her."

Both hands moved against his temples, pressing the clean cuts of his gentleman's haircut. The curls sitting atop his head fell down into his face, blurring my view of his unsteady eyes.

Rolling my lip ring between my teeth, I watched his attention return to the openness of the cafe, lost in the emotion digging up this memory had brought with it. "Did you love her?"

"Does it matter?" His head rolled back to me, more tense than before. "No one deserves to be treated like that. Who does that to someone?" He shook his head before settling down between his drooping shoulders. "She spent three years of her life with me, and I tore it down like it was nothing. It wasn't nothing. I . . . I guess it doesn't matter what it was now."

The strings of my heart wrapped around itself, stifling the blood from entering and exiting the chambers that kept my body alive. I bit my tongue to keep my eyes from breaking. A roaring sea of memories crashed inside my skull. He was like Paul. But unlike Paul, he showed remorse. Regret. The hurt was clear in every word spoken and every movement he made. How sorry he was; I didn't think it was possible to be that way.

"Why . . ." I swallowed. "Why are you telling me this?"

"I don't know." He wiped his finger across his nose, sniffling loudly before looking at me again. "You seemed like someone who would understand. Somehow."

My heart was strangled at this point. I did understand. All too well. Only I was on the opposite end of it. I was the victim. Did Paul regret what he did? No. He wouldn't. He enjoyed every second he held me under his thumb. And I let him. Because I was too scared. Even when I smashed a glass against his face and left him reeling, I was petrified. It didn't change how afraid I was. It only made it worse.

A thought popped into my head as we remained across from the other. How did Ameel know I'd understand? Did he know Paul? Did he put him up to this? No. There's no way. Krish brought him into my life, not a psychotic ex-boyfriend.

The entire cafe seemed to close in around me, slowly cracking my bones into tiny fragments left to litter my insides and damage the inner workings of my physical form. I was glad Ameel somberly stared into his cup, watching the steady movement of the liquid as I squeezed my hands in between my thighs to keep myself from shaking. Trying to recover any resemblance of control was impossible. I was there again, standing in the kitchen, allowing my oppressor to suck the life from me with every word.

How could Ameel know? That I was a mirror of the victim to his retaliation against commitment? It could all be bullshit. Maybe he was an actor playing a part. I couldn't know for sure. It felt genuine, but I couldn't be sure. This is what happened when I dropped my guard for even a second. Whoever it may be, they would find a way to worm in.

There was more being uncovered than I bargained for. This wasn't just about finding out what kept Krish tethered to this life. Not anymore.

WALKING to work the next day, I found myself kicking rocks and stones into the shallow shoreline. It was almost midday, and the sun was shrouded in a haze of whisking clouds, moving faster than the wind could blow. I had my pink and black knit hat pulled over my ears and my leopard print scarf wrapped clumsily at my neck. Fur trimmed boots overlapped my patterned leg warmers, keeping my feet dry if I happened to step into the water.

Krish kept pace with me, his hands in his pockets, hanging like an article of clothing on a clothes hanger. We didn't talk much after Ameel's confession. I had nothing much to say about it, only that I still didn't know what to make of it. Was he being honest? It was easy to believe in the moment, but now that time had passed, doubt spread over it like a pool of blood across a white linoleum floor. Even if it were the truth, no amount of scrubbing could hide what doubt had already embedded in my mind.

"The conversation with Ameel," Krish's voice was riddled with cracks and a hoarseness that matched his diminishing form. "It must not have been easy for him to tell you what he did."

Tucking my chin into my scarf, I pulled at the fingers of my winter patterned gloves. "It's bullshit."

"Why do you say that?"

"Why would he tell me?" I stopped at the bottom of the stone stairwell leading up to the street and faced him. "A complete stranger? There's only one reason for it."

Krish yanked on his hole-ridden blazer. "And what would that reason be?"

Saying what I wanted to say would sound childish. Rolling my tongue over the metal of my lip ring, I shrugged as my arms folded against my chest. "All men lie. It's how they get what they want."

"Do you truly believe that?" Even though I've told Krish bits and pieces of my life before escaping Paul, there was still so much to divulge that I just couldn't dig up. It was buried, and that's where it needed to remain.

"You did not see what I saw," Krish continued. "His aura was in turmoil. Hues shifting and changing with despair and a longing to be heard. This was something he had not confessed to anyone. It was painful for him."

The gremlins stacked bricks and stone along the top of my walls with every word he said. I knew he was probably right, but there was no real way for me to know. Krish could be making it up so I wouldn't abandon this frail attempt at answers. He could be using me, too.

"How do I know that? Because you told me?" I started walking up the stairs, stopping after the first three or four before turning around again. "Look. I don't even know if you're really a ghost. You could be a figment of my imagination. My subconscious trying to force me to break down the walls I built around myself. For good reasons."

"And?" Krish's hand fluttered to the railing and grasped it. "What if I am? What is it you are so afraid to face, Raina?"

I leaned against the railing in my attempt to justify my defenses. "He's just like my ex. Treating his girlfriend like she didn't matter. I didn't matter. I didn't even have a voice! He ran my life and showed me off like some prize he'd won, dressing me up how *he* wanted me to be."

With a quick turn, I made my way up the stairs to the street. My stomach was in knots and nausea soon coated the back of my throat. Just saying that much made my skin crawl. I hated remembering. I hated having to remember.

"Your feelings are genuine," Krish's voice came from behind me. "That man had no right to take your humanity from you."

As we arrived on the street by the cafe, Krish reached for my arm, turning me around to face him. "But does that condemn every other person from getting close to you for the rest of your life?"

"*Yes*. It does." It hurt to admit that out loud. Ignoring the truth in that statement was easier than facing the fear that created it. I wish I wasn't this way, but it was impossible to wrangle myself free from it. I was still in the trap, writhing and twisting myself to get free. But the more I struggled, the deeper the teeth sank into my bones.

Krish's hand relaxed on my arm, the steady pulse of his presence sent waves of calm through my rattled body. "I understand you are fearful."

"Krish," I whispered as I shook my head. "You don't know anything about being afraid."

His eyes sunk farther into his sockets after hearing my words. Unkempt hair broke free and fell where it pleased. "Perhaps you are right." His hand dropped from my arm. "I am only saying what I feel to be my truth. That is all I have now."

A dense swallow dropped the nausea back down into the pit of my stomach. I didn't mean to sound offensive or accuse him of not having feelings. But no one could understand unless they've walked in my shoes. It was impossible to know how much fear could rule your life unless you lived it.

"Hey." I looked up and found Ameel trotting over to me. He was wearing his usual dark knit jacket and jeans. The curls bounced on top of his head as he came to a halt a few feet from where I stood. "I thought I'd find you here."

Seeing him elevated my blood pressure to almost bursting levels. I squinted, trying to control the urge to scream as loud as I could.

"Look. I can't talk long. I got a work thing. But I just wanted to say I'm sorry for unloading on you the other day."

"It was bullshit." My voice was harsh and accusing, cutting through the air like a knife.

Ameel drew his head back in surprise. "What?"

"What you said. About your girlfriend?" My arms went rigid at my sides. "It was all bullshit."

"It wasn't bullshit." His arms came up with his shoulders. "Why would I make something like that up?"

"I can think of a few reasons."

"Name one."

I could feel my heart beating faster and faster with every passing second. "To butter me up. Make me feel sorry for you. So you can get in my head or pants, most likely."

"Wow," he scoffed, shaking his head. "No offense, but you are the last person I would try that with."

"More incentive. You think I'm easy."

"What the hell is your deal? Is this how you treat everyone you come in contact with? Or is it just me? *Or*," he leaned in on his heels towards me, "is it a guy thing?"

I twisted my mouth into a knot and tightened my jaw. I could feel a rush of emotion washing over me, drowning my surging anger in the waves of my unbridled despair. With a weary sigh, I hugged my arms to my chest in an attempt to keep myself from falling apart. "I have my reasons."

"Reasons that justify you treating people like shit, huh?" Ameel's hand came up the side of his head and rested on his curly top. "I guess we're the same in that."

He paced back and forth, from the edge of the street toward the sidewalk. I watched him, still keeping my arms wrapped around me. I could feel Krish standing behind me, and I was glad for it. If I fell, he would catch me.

"Fuck it." Ameel threw his hands up. "I don't know why I bothered. What am I even doing . . . " With a deep breath, he turned away from me with his hands on his hips, staring down the street as a few cars and people continued on with their day. "Whatever." Backing up, he looked at me. "I'm done. See you never, Ariel. Have a nice life."

WE MADE our way to the gallery in silence. Krish stayed close to me. I could feel his tattered clothing brush against my jacketed arm every now and again. It wasn't a physical touch that I felt, but a chill. So cold and hopeless, it numbed me down to my bones. Gritting my teeth was the only way I could keep it at bay. But as we walked further, I was beginning to be numb to it, like it was becoming part of me.

Walking into the gallery, I was greeted by my boss with a well-groomed smile. My boss was a rather tall fellow, with slicked back hair and a genuine approachability I couldn't explain. He always dressed well, and his wife, who was co-owner of the gallery, kept up appearances.

I took my place behind the front desk, seeing the stack of papers I would need to go through that day. The gallery was preparing for a spring exhibition, featuring newer artists from all over New England. My job was to make sure all the artwork was shipped and received appropriately, as well as keeping social channels up-to-date with artist information, special invites, and weekly sneak peeks. When the boss was here, he took care of the visitors for the most part, leaving me uninterrupted in my work. It was a lot to do, but I loved keeping busy.

Krish wearily slumped down on the floor behind my desk, bringing his knees up to rest his head. Straggly dark hair hung down onto his dirtied slacks as a heavy sigh rose and fell from his graying frame.

"Krish," I whispered as I glanced down at him. "I'm sorry."

"You are doing all you can." His gaze found mine. "What more is there?"

My mind wandered to a ton of possibilities, all of which I did not wish to partake in. If I never saw Ameel again, then this was all for nothing. There were no other signs Krish had given me that there was another option.

"I'll find Ameel again." I sighed. "I hate seeing you like this. You're falling apart."

There was no response as Krish sank back against the wall with his eyes clamped shut. I don't think he would admit he was in any sort of pain. Do ghosts feel pain? Maybe emptiness.

"Raina."

My boss's voice interrupted my train of thought as my eyes shot open. He wasn't alone. Ameel's hand slid across the counter of my desk, coming to a stop a foot or so from my computer. My eyes widened with shock as I tried desperately to keep my heart from jumping out of my throat.

"Raina, this is Ameel Javed. He's the videographer who'll be shooting our next exhibition." I heard my boss talking, but I couldn't stop myself from staring at Ameel's polite expression. My boss's brow rose, the corner of his mouth curling into the pockets of his cheekbones. "Raina?"

I blinked a few times before finding my boss's curious stare. The blurred form of Krish popped up in my peripheral view. "Yes. Okay. But . . . don't you usually shoot the exhibitions? I didn't know you were bringing someone else in."

"I think it's time for a change, don't you? Give us more to work with now that we have to worry about social media marketing. Besides, we're getting some bigger names this year." He placed a warm hand on Ameel's shoulder. "Raina will take all your information. You'll be working with her directly up until the event."

"Sounds good." Ameel's lips parted to reveal his charmingly alluring smile. "I look forward to working with you."

A cough caught in my throat as I failed to keep my posture steady. "Likewise."

"Well, I'll leave you to it. Why don't you give him a tour of the gallery? It's not as big as others you'll find, but it's got character." With a final glance, my boss left Ameel standing in front of me, his arms rested on the desk as he leaned in toward my computer.

"What are you doing here?" was my gut response once I was clear from prying ears.

He shrugged. "Working. I'm the videographer, or did you miss that part of the conversation?"

"Did you know you were coming here?"

"Yeah, but I didn't know *you* would be here."

My toes began to curl in my boots as I shifted my eyes, not knowing where to focus. Krish looked as surprised as I did, which brought life back into his withering face.

Clearing my throat, I pulled up the contacts for the exhibition and added a new entry. "Well, I need your information."

"It's all on my card."

With a single motion, his hand slid across the counter, landing next to my keyboard. Instinctually, I reached out to take it, landing on the surface of his fingers. My attention flashed to him and we lingered there for a second, neither one moving nor willing to pull away. For some reason, I couldn't think or act. The blood rushing through my veins intensified faster than if I were running a marathon. It kept time in my ears and against my chest, counting down the seconds that we allowed this to continue.

Finally, as if somehow communicating without words, we each drew away from the other. Slowly, so that not an inch of touched skin would go unnoticed. Even though it was only the top of his fingers, they were soft like velvet. His rings breaking the connection between us for only a millisecond, but a millisecond I unconsciously wished I could have back.

I grasped on to his card like I needed it to live, my heart slowly coming back down to normalcy. Ameel's arms came off the counter. He scratched the back of his neck; his once concentrated eyes now scanning the floor for answers. I didn't need him to say a word. Not a single sound to know that he was trapped by whatever it was that had come over us just as strongly as I was.

"Thank you . . . Aladdin," I whispered as I placed the card against my screen, barely able to make out the words.

"Sure."

I typed his information in silence, unable to blink or look at him again. Out of the corner of my eye, he was shifting around. Keeping his feet moving, probably to distract himself. The air was stripped of the usual tension I felt around him. Now it was anxious, scary maybe. Like something we both never wanted to happen, had or was about to.

After inputting all his information, I led him around the gallery, explaining how things would go for the exhibition. My voice was on auto-pilot to his one-word responses. The wittiness and smugness were completely absent from his tone. I, too, could not think of a single thing to fall back on. It didn't help that the closer I was to him, the more my lungs fell short of breath. When the tour was over, I walked him to the door.

"I'll send you more information for the exhibit once I get it all together," I said as straightforward as I could force myself to. "The planning meeting is in two weeks."

"Right, I'll be there." His hands sat in his pockets, head hanging slightly, forcing his eyes to dart upward to look at me.

I wanted to touch him again, but the urge was so unnatural it froze me to the floor. "Listen, Aladdin . . . " I glanced back into the gallery, seeing Krish sitting on one of the benches. His sullen gaze fixed on us. "About before."

"It's okay." Ameel straightened his posture and took a nervous breath. "Don't worry about it."

"No, it's just …" My hands started to clam up as I gripped my clipboard. "I didn't mean to call you a liar. I do . . . believe you. I just …"

"You don't have to say anything." A weak smile graced his face, rippling the hairs of my arms.

"Okay."

We stood there; me watching him and him watching me. The soft brown of his eyes searching my features like he was admiring a fine piece of art. Nerves shot through me, rapidly expediting the rush of euphoria to my heart. Then he took a slow step forward, narrowing the gap between us. I clutched my clipboard like I wanted it to become part of me, breathing in the Old Spice scent I secretly desired. But then Ameel seemed to catch himself, leaning back toward the door.

"Bye, Ariel."

Faster than my mind could comprehend, he was out the door. As it slowly closed, meeting with the doorframe, I caught a breath in my lungs and held it there.

Walking as fast as I could, I raced towards the bathroom, shutting the door before falling behind it. Krish was already sitting on the bleached tile in front of me, as my head fell in between my hands. Our connection replayed in my head over and over again. I didn't understand it, how this smart-ass had completely derailed me like a love-struck idiot. My heart had yet to recover from emotions I didn't even know I still had. How I wanted to be close to him, touch him, even knowing that he was a lying, rotten cheater.

"Raina." Krish's voice was a breath of the wind. "Raina."

My eyes fell to his. As weary as they were, there was a flash of newness in them. "It was stronger. The memory." His hand came up with weak intent, grasping at the hazy air surrounding him. "When your hands met, I could almost reach out and touch it. What I've lost. It's there. Just beyond."

There was madness in his tone as his hands came on mine. The graying aurora surrounding him began to darken against his closed eyes. His lips trembled, and I was afraid he would fall apart into a thousand tiny pieces. "The water . . . like mirrors catching the sunlight. Cast upon a pale blue. Something at the bow. Beckoning me with precious light. From eyes I cannot see ..."

His hands began to burn mine. So intensely, my flight response bowed away from him, backing into the corner of the bathroom. No amount of air could quell the need to escape from my racing mind. I watched as his color continued to swell, reaching up toward the intense lights nestled in the ceiling, coating them completely in an ominous haze. He didn't seem to notice I wasn't there, hands still hovering to where he had met mine.

For a moment, I was frozen by the ever-growing darkness that slowly consumed every inch of the bathroom. Darting my gaze from one stretch to the other, I finally came back to the crouched form of Krish, still stagnant in his position and darkening posture. His eyes were a hollow void with nothing left to hold on to.

Biting my lip ring, I lunged forward on sheer willpower. His burning palms met my cold, distressed fingers as I shook them uncontrollably. "Snap out of it. *Krish!*"

Nothing changed. Panic moved my hold to his face, which seemed to come away beneath my fingers. Tossing my hair to the side, I tried to stay focused and not let fear get the better of me. "Krish. It's Raina. Please come back to me. I need you to come back."

The holes where his eyes once were expanded. In less than a second, the form returned to them, shooting open with confused clarity. The fog subsided like he had sucked it back into his ghostly form. His eyes were colorless until the final mist had returned to him, filling the whites with the dark brown he once possessed.

"What happened?" he asked, grasping my hands with such force I thought he'd break my fingers. "What did I do?"

"It's okay. It's gonna be okay."

"Did I hurt you? I . . . I don't remember."

"*Krish*." The sharp tone I rarely adopted struck focus onto his face. He watched me. The lines of his face deepened and his complexion deteriorated before my very eyes. How I was keeping myself from screaming bloody murder, I had no idea. As terrified as I was, he looked equally, if not more. This was scarier for him than me. *And he didn't know fear. What's wrong with me?* I had to be the one to keep it together. Because he was falling apart.

"It's okay. We . . . " Swallowing the subsiding panic, I tried to keep myself in control. "We'll figure it out. We're almost there."

"We are?"

My legs trembled under my body. I had no clue if what I was saying was true. But I had to lie. To keep him from becoming whatever darkness was trying to take him. I didn't know if I could save him. I didn't even know what *this* was. All I knew is that when I touched Ameel, something happened that stirred the pot of whatever ghost story I was forced to be a part of. It was the only thing I had to go on. Maybe this was the answer. The question was, could I force myself to endure memories I wished I could forget, if only to save Krish's soul from becoming something monstrous.

It wasn't until now that I realized how much I didn't want Krish to leave my side. I took advantage of his presence and what it had given me. I was finally heard, finally recognized. Everything I've been through, he never pushed it aside or made an excuse for why it happened or how I felt. I couldn't let whatever it was that was trying to destroy him take him away. No matter what. I had to break the pattern before it was too late.

"Yes." I forced a weak smile, which he matched the moment it graced my lips. "We are."

"LISTEN." Krish placed his hands on my shoulders, gliding me to a halt as we walked toward the cafe. "I will not ask you to do something you do not want to do."

Gritting my teeth, I bit my lower lip, letting the metal ring slide across my teeth. "It's too late. I already texted him. It's happening."

I spent those last few days wracking my brain over what the next steps were. My mind and my heart were not in sync at all. Logically, I wanted to run as fast as humanly possible from this situation. I have never been so scared and confused in my entire life. Everything was happening faster than I could comprehend. But time was not on my side. If I didn't act now, Krish would die again. Or become a demon. It didn't matter *what* he would become, only that I had to stop it from happening.

And Ameel. As much as I wanted to hate him, I could not ignore the effect touching him had on me. It changed my analogy of his character. Made me want to know more about him. Get close to him, both physically and emotionally. And the fact that he was also acting strange because of it . . . There wasn't a clearer message that something was happening.

Crossing the sunlit street, we were almost to the shoreline where Beans n' Cream would be waiting for us. Despite the extra layer of sushi printed socks on my feet, I could barely feel my toes. My hands pulled at the loose lumps of wool on my knitted tunic. The tassels of my leopard scarf wafted behind me, animating the quickness of my pace. It was all or nothing. Krish's chance rode on my cooperation, and that twisted my stomach into more knots than I could count.

I stopped just as we were about to enter the cafe. "Krish." I looked at him. "I'm sorry I've been so selfish."

He placed a weary hand on my shoulder. "There is nothing you need to be sorry for, but thank you." His bony fingers squeezed gently. "You are strong, Raina. It is your greatest gift."

My lips rolled back into my mouth, sucking down the sudden emotion from creeping up on me. This was the time where I needed my strength the most.

As we walked through the cafe door, my eyes fell directly to the back of Ameel's head. He turned around the second my entire body was safely on the other side of the doors. My heart skipped a beat as his shining, dark eyes fell on me.

"Raina," Krish's voice tumbled to my ear.

"I'm fine," I whispered after a deep breath propelled me forward. Dark fit jeans matched Ameel's favorite footwear. A white Ziggy Stardust tee sat underneath the unbuttoned folds of his blue flannel. He neatly combed his curls back, but a few strands hung from the sides almost intentionally.

"Hey." He followed me to the chair across from him, which I took with subtle caution. "I ordered your signature chai already."

"Thanks." I slipped my sloth bag over the chair.

Krish hovered behind me, waiting like a cloud of cigarette smoke. I could sense the fear gently wafting from the gray flickers of his haunting. My fingers tapped against the wooden table. I wasn't even sure what I was going to do. Only that I needed to see Ameel and figure out what the hell this was.

Ameel looked at me with an uncertain gaze. A heaviness encapsulated my chest the longer we sat in silence amongst the clinking of ceramic mugs and the light chattering of other patrons.

With a quick sigh, he folded his hands in front of him. "I was surprised to get your text."

I curled my fingers between my legs, almost too terrified to look at him. "Yeah, well. I . . . have to tell you something."

"Is it about the gallery?"

"No." I forced my gaze, even though the gremlins were threatening to empty anything that remained of my breakfast out through my mouth.

"What is it?"

All the nerve endings throughout my body were shooting off rockets across my skin. I opened my mouth, but no words came out. The sounds of the cafe seemed to escalate, making it harder for me to concentrate on anything resembling a conversation. My heart was beating so fast I couldn't count how many times it knocked against my chest.

"There's . . . something following me." My words lingered between us, cementing our uncertainty.

"A ghost."

My eyes widened. "Yes, but it's more than that."

"Here you two go." The barista placed our orders on the table before us. There wasn't enough logical sense left in me to even muster a cordial response. Ameel and I stayed locked in each other's gaze as the barista stepped away from our table. "Enjoy."

Ameel looked down at his wafting cup of joe. "Listen, Ariel ..." he said with a breathless sigh as his eyes met mine again.

"No. Wait." I didn't know what to make of what was said, only that there was something I needed to do first before I could fully understand everything that was happening.

"I was with someone." I could feel my hands begin to shake, so I wrapped them around the warm, wafting mug of vanilla chai, watching the cream and cinnamon swirl into unpredictable patterns.

"He was . . . " I swallowed hard, trying to muster up the strength Krish saw in me to help push through this. "He told me how to act. What to wear. I looked how he wanted me to look and did what he wanted me to do. I lost myself in his illusion of what he saw me to be. Lost without a voice of my own."

My eyes wandered up to face Ameel. He watched me intently, hands still folded in front of him, a sharp line replacing his mouth. "I was afraid of what he would do if I defied him. If he'd hurt me or worse. When I finally got away, I thought I wouldn't be afraid anymore. That I'd finally be free. But I'm still afraid. Even more than when I was with him."

Ameel held his last breath tight within his chest. "What's his name?"

My face furrowed in confusion. "What?"

"What's his name? I swear to God, I'll beat the shit out of him."

I shook my head. "No. I . . . I don't want that."

He leaned forward. "Who is he, Ariel?"

"*Stop.*" My hands fell flat on the table. "I didn't tell you so you could do something stupid. I told you because . . . " I bit my tongue. He listened, but only to what Paul had done to me. Not about what the aftershock had been.

Standing up, I pushed the chair out from under me and grabbed my bag, throwing it onto my shoulder. "I need to go."

"No. Wait." Ameel reached for me as I hurried for the door.

Bursting through the door like a bull, my pulse echoed in my ears, sending a numbing shiver down my spine. Fear grabbed me by the hair and was pulling me as far away from that corner cafe as possible.

It's too much. I can't do it. I can't.

My feet hit the concrete laid staircase leading down to the snow-kissed shore. I never wanted to be invisible, even when I was. But now, I'd give anything to switch places with Krish. To let the darkness take me away and everything I was running from.

THE WATER BARELY RIPPLED, like glass reflecting hints of light that dared to hit. Krish fluttered around me like a tornado, disrupting the stillness of my empty stare at the rocky sand beneath my feet.

"Raina. Raina, please stop."

Shaking my head, I gripped onto the strap of my bag, pulling it tight against my shoulder. "I can't. I'm so sorry, Krish."

"Yes, you can."

"No." I turned around to face his pulsing form. "I'm afraid . . . I'm so . . . fucking scared."

Krish's boney fingers grasped my shoulders. "If you let that keep you in one place, you will miss countless chances that could be something more. Something greater. You deserve to live a life without fear."

Dropping my head, I could feel dry emotion forcing condensation to build up behind my eyes. "It's not that simple."

"You cannot fly if you do not jump."

I looked up into Krish's gaunt cheeks and exhaust laden eyes. "If I don't jump, I won't fall! I won't get hurt anymore."

Krish's hands ran down my arm. "We must fall to understand what it means to live. To be present." His shadowy grip sent a strange, icy sensation into my wrists. "I am sorry for what you had to go through. But you are not alone anymore. You need to let the past go. Jump."

"Never" meant nothing would go wrong. That was what I chose to live by since escaping that life of confinement and fear. If I never let anyone in, I'd be okay. If I never tried, I wouldn't fail. If I never forgave, I would have something to hold on to. But that something was remorse and contempt, all bad things that ate you alive from the inside out. That sounded ignorant and foolish to me now. All because a dead person flipped my life upside down. Because he pushed me to save him by saving myself.

"Raina."

A faint voice barely broke Krish's concentration, but I followed his gaze behind me as he dropped my hands to turn. Ameel stood before me, nerves rattling his fingers as they played in his palms.

"I . . . I didn't mean to say that. If it upset you—"

"What was her name?" My voice shook with uncertainty. I could feel the seams coming apart at my sides. Everything I had kept buried inside me for so long, threatening to pour out.

"What?"

"Her name." I took in a rattled breath. "Your girlfriend."

Ameel pressed his hands together, bracing himself. We waited there, staring at each other as light snowflakes began to trickle down from the sky.

"Raina . . . " Krish's voice trailed off as a fog began to drift across the snow-flurried sand. I didn't need to see what was happening; I felt it like a storm. Krish fell to his knees beside me, the darkness leaking out of him like a waterfall. "I . . . "

The hair on my arms tickled my skin as my nerves re-lived the terror they felt on the floor of the bathroom. I kept my gaze on Ameel, still waiting for something to happen. Not knowing something *was* happening. Beyond anyone's control.

"Melanie." The name fell from his lips like a stone. He let out a nervous huff. "God. I haven't said her name out loud since—"

"Since it happened?"

His body settled. "Yeah."

The darkness leaking from Krish stained the sand beneath my feet. I couldn't look at it. I had to stay focused on Ameel. Or I'd run away all over again.

"Mine was Paul." His name was the trigger I had feared to pull, sending tears streaming from the overflowing sea behind my eyes. "Paul ..." I hung my head, watching the blackness creep up my boots. But there was no fear. Not after muttering that name.

"I *hate* you." I gritted my teeth as my hair fell into my face, watching tears crash into the pool of shadows lapping at my feet. "I hate what you took from me. I wish I'd never met you. I wish I'd never fallen in love with you. You broke my spirit. My life it's . . . so broken."

Something collided with me, creating a safety net around my entire person. BearGlove flooded my nostrils, igniting my senses in a warmth I had long since forgotten. Ameel tightened his arms around me, leaning his face against my head, his lips resting inches from my ear.

"I'm sorry. You didn't deserve to be treated like that. Like you meant nothing. You meant everything to me. I just . . . " I could feel his chin quivering against my temples.

"I was so scared. And that's not an excuse. There is no excuse for what I did. You deserved better. So much better. I wish I could take it all back. I hurt you so badly. I just . . . I'm sorry. Melanie, I'm so sorry."

Closing my eyes, I buried my head against his chest, clutching onto him like if I let go, I'd fall into oblivion. My chest tightened as my body relaxed in his arms, using the safety between them as the only catalyst for my strength.

"I forgive you, Paul. I forgive you."

A light burst beneath us, scattering across the sand like a skipping stone. I broke away from Ameel, both of us stepping in opposite directions as the light expanded. It eradicated the darkness consuming Krish's melting form. My hands clutched against my chest as Krish rose from the sand. His once-darkening silhouette refreshed in a now white glow, enhancing his vibrancy and reigniting the youthfulness he once possessed. I squinted as a final burst exploded from him, feeling the shock wave of light pass through me.

When the haze finally dissipated, Krish stood before me, admiring his renewed self with a smile tickling his lips. He looked at me, his handsome face no longer shrouded in gray. He was alive again.

"Krish."

Both of us looked in Ameel's direction, who stood beside a form drenched in blue light. I took a step back as it began to come away, outlining the flow of ebony tendrils against a beautifully crafted profile. A long coral dress pulsed to life, cascading down to a pair of daintily slippered feet. I stared at this now fully embodied woman, who could not keep her brilliantly lit eyes from Krish's astonished gaze.

"Fiona," Krish muttered.

My hands covered my quivering chin as small pockets of tears continued to fall from my eyes. Fiona gave a warm smile as she sailed forward, meeting Krish in-between Ameel and me. Krish took her hands gingerly, as if unsure she was really there.

"Krish." Fiona's fingers reached for his face, gracing his cheek. "I . . . I remember you."

The two embraced, each holding on so tightly in fear that they may lose each other all over again. My gaze darted to Ameel, who stood stoically in awe at their reunion. When he noticed me, he smiled, expediting the pattering of my heart.

"Your hair in the wind as we crossed the Hudson. How could I forget? You stopped my heart with a single glance," Krish muttered as he leaned his forehead against hers. "But I've found you."

Krish turned to me with grateful satisfaction as they broke

from one another. I didn't hesitate in my stride to meet him, his arms safely cradling me against his now warm, comforting glow. Burying my face in his chest, my tears seemed to pass right through him as he steadied my shuttering frame.

"Thank you, Raina." I looked up at his beaming smile, smelling the sweet perfume of his joy. "You saved me."

Wiping a stray tear from my face, I let the warm spark of his touch refresh my skin. "I don't want you to leave."

Krish brushed my tears away with his thumb as his continued smile came next to my ear. "I will always be with you." A gentle kiss touched down on my cheek. Coming back to meet my gaze, his arms loosened around me. "You are finally free."

I felt my face bend to his, creating a joyfulness inside me I never knew I had. "We're both free." His arms fall, clutching my hands one final time. "I'll never forget you."

"It's time. To live your life now." His fingers slipped from mine as he moved away.

I glanced at Ameel. Fiona was in his ear, whispering something before placing a kiss on his forehead. The action closed his eyes with a quiet serenity, as she came to meet Krish with her hand, ready to accept him.

I stepped back, watching them turn toward the sea. At the shoreline, the dull light masked by the clouds soon parted, giving way to a brilliant pathway to the sky. Krish and Fiona faded into the gently lapping water, hand in hand, sparkling against the sun's rays until there was nothing left but the endless horizon. Silence took hold for a few trailing moments. I waited, secretly longing for them to come back. But I knew they wouldn't. They'd found the light.

With a shaky hand, I wiped the wetness from my face, sucking in a harsh breath as I turned toward Ameel. He looked at me, both of us unsure what to even do or say. My heart felt still, anticipating the start of something bigger than I had ever experienced.

"When you said ghost at the cafe." I choked up momentarily, letting a few more tears escape. "You meant it."

Ameel nodded, remaining quiet in the aftermath of the moment.

"I don't think they were ghosts." A soft smile graced my cheeks.

"No." His gaze strayed toward the sea. "They were angels." A glisten of sadness fell down his cheek before he lowered his head with a sigh. "You know, you're the bravest person I've ever met." His eyes came up to meet mine, now shuttering like a turbulent sea, at words I never thought I'd hear anyone say.

"So . . . I guess . . . I guess, I'll see ya."

He started to walk away, the back of his head slowly becoming the worst sight I could ever see. For a second, I couldn't move or speak, but I pushed for it. Because I wouldn't let anything hold me back. Deep in my mind, I knew it wasn't love. But I needed Ameel. In what way, I wasn't sure. This experience brought us together, two people who would never have done so on our own. I wanted to find out why, and, I hoped to Krish, he wanted to find out, too.

"Ameel." The call of his name from my lips stopped him, and he turned around to face me. "Do you like . . . breakfast?"

A grin flashed across his face. "Yeah."

I pressed my hand into my palm. "Would you like to . . . go get breakfast with me tomorrow?"

His smile grew, flashing his pearly whites in my direction. "Yeah. I'd like that." He gestured with his head down the street. "You heading to work?"

I nodded softly. "Yeah. In a bit."

"I'll walk you. If you don't mind—"

"No. I mean, yes." I scurried over, taking a stand beside him. "I don't mind." Impulse allowed me to take his hand in mine, matched with little resistance. "Thank you."

"For what?"

"For . . . everything."

My smile matched his own as I moved to release his hand. But Ameel's grasp caught mine, keeping me tethered to him. "You don't have to let go. If you don't want to." I laced my fingers between his, stepping in closer, unable to pull myself from his dark eyes as the snow continued to fall around us. "Shall we move on?"

"Yeah." I leaned into my first step with him beside me. "I'm ready."

3 Months Later...

THE GALLERY WAS BUSTLING with artists from all across New England, dressed for the Ceres Spring Exhibition. The walls were lined with new and unique pieces. From abstract patterns to color filled landscapes to poetic obscurity that captured the newness of the season.

My hair changed from mermaid blue to a fiery red, neatly combed and done up in a right sided bun. Exhibitions called for a classier style, so I found a very whimsical knee length, slate blue dress in a second hand store that seemed to dance in the wind with every turn of my head.

It was well into the exhibition, people roaming both inside and out of the gallery. Hors d'oeuvres and champagne were being served outside the doors, but plenty of people carried them in and around the gallery as they chatted up the artists and shared smiles of adoration.

I stood proudly in the third display space beside the windows, my hands folded behind my back. Six paintings decorated the wall behind me. Paintings created by my own hand, fueled by my supernatural experience. My boss was more than thrilled to have them in the show, wanting me to paint a series after I showed him the initial piece. And so I worked tirelessly in the short months I had up to the show until I had six completed. Now they were here, sitting amongst works by some of the most well known artists in New England.

"These are stunning!" One artist spoke when they were first displayed. "Such emotion captured in every stroke."

I still wasn't used to the compliments. Juggling being a featured artist as well as making sure everything was running smoothly was taking a tole on me, even this early in the day. But luckily my boss was taking the reins on this one, telling me to enjoy myself and focus on being an artist.

After chatting up a few more visitors, I took a deep breath, leaning against the side of the window. I closed my eyes to try and focus on any small bit of silence I could to clear my head from all the excitement. All the attention, it was overwhelming.

"Artist life too much for you?"

I didn't need to open my eyes to know Ameel was smiling ear to ear, but it was a nice first sight to see once I did. He had his camera equipment in hand, wearing dark jeans with a matching dark tee and sport coat. His hair was neatly combed, with a few stray curls threatening to break away from the front.

"I'm not used to this at all."

"Need a break?" He lowered his camera, which was securely strapped across his chest. Reaching out his hand, he took mine, "Come on. Let's get some air."

Every time our fingers met, a rush of euphoria raised the goosebumps across my skin. Like I was riding the most dangerous wave in the ocean or falling from the moon back down to earth. It was constant, even after months had past since I first experienced it. It was never anything more than this, but it was the most intense and exhilarating feeling I had ever felt. Anything more scared me too much to indulge in. Though I couldn't pretend the thought had never crossed my mind.

We slipped through the gallery and out the front door. My boss was standing at the entrance and smiled as we passed, placing a hand on my shoulder as we stepped onto the street. We passed the tents and tables that were set up in front and crossed to the other side. Our hands left each other as the water came into view. The fresh salty air of the harbor filled my lungs and refreshed my spirit. With eyes closed, I took in a lungful before letting it trickle out of my nose.

"Better?"

"Yeah." I turned to Ameel. "Much better."

We stood together, letting the muted sounds of seagulls and water breaking across the wooden docks cover the silence between us. The corner of his lip twitched into a smirk before looking out onto the shore. "Do you still think about them?"

I nodded, joining him in his vigil. "Yeah. All the time."

Krish was a constant thought. There were days I still glanced outside my window, hoping he'd be under the streetlamp, waiting for me. I wanted to know where he went or how he was. If he was even conscious of himself or the person he lived as. These questions I couldn't imagine being answered. But I hoped, whatever became of him, that he was at peace. I missed him, but as much as I wanted him beside me, I didn't feel alone anymore. Not after everything and everyone.

"You look amazing by the way."

I looked at Ameel with a smirk, his gaze catching mine. "More like Ariel?"

"Yeah, but way, *way* prettier."

I felt my cheeks flush, the sudden flattery melting into a smile. My feet shifted as I cast my eyes to the pebble speckled street. Ameel had become something of a confidant. We both shared something that not many people would ever hope of experiencing. Something spiritual and fueled by raw emotion. We respected each other and told each other things I wouldn't tell anyone, not even my brothers. I trusted him more than myself sometimes, not knowing if that was because of what we shared or because of something more.

"Hey, can I tell you something?"

I looked at him, nodding my head quietly. Ameel rocked on his heels, taking a step closer. "Remember when I first came to the gallery and... you touched my hand on the counter?"

My heart was already pounding, remembering how much that touch ignited life back into my bones. "Yeah."

"I know something happened then. I felt it happen. I *still* feel it happening. Every time I take your hand." Slowly, he reached for mine again, letting his fingers tickle the tips of my fingers before they folded into his. "I know you feel it too."

There it was again. The wave washing over me like water over a parched desert. The only comparison would be the joy I felt in Krish's arms before he faded into the horizon. How calm and content he was and how much it made me want that for myself.

I pressed my lips together, the coolness of my lip ring helping me keep my focus. "Did you want to kiss me? At the door before you left?"

Ameel waited a few seconds, keeping his soft brown eyes on my grayish blue. "I did. But I was scared. I didn't know why." He paused. "I didn't understand a lot of things back then."

"Back then." I grinned. "Like it was years ago."

"Feels like it was."

"Yeah. It does." I looked down at our connection. His sand tainted fingers intertwined with my pale white. It felt right, being here with him. It always felt right. Sometimes for reasons I didn't understand. But who needed to understand *everything*? That was one of the most meaningful things I could have learned from Krish. To be able to move forward without needing to fully understand how my life would unfold.

Meeting Ameel's gaze again, I squeezed his hand tightly. "Are you still scared?"

"Always." He tugged to draw me closer. "But I'd kiss you. If you'd let me."

My heart skipped a few beats as his Old Spice scent mixed with the salty air. He wasn't Paul. But that fear still lingered that everything would go terribly wrong. I couldn't think about the *what if's*. Because I knew what I wanted. In the moment. "And ... if I let you?"

"I guess we'll find out."

Another test. Another moment to live in fully and wholeheartedly. I didn't want to let it slip away. Not now. Not ever.

I closed the gap between me and my Arabian knight. The soft feel of his lips on mine instantly flooded my insides, my mind swimming and rolling in and out with the tide. His other hand lightly graced my jawline as we became fully consumed in the moment. Both of us parting and coming together, never begging for it to cease, but diving deeper and moving closer, trying to become part of the other. It collapsed my lungs and stifled my heart.

We had both been lead through the shadows of our own making by the wings of angels and now, we were soaring in the light. With the same unmatched love that connected Krish and Fiona, both in life and in death.

Acknowledgments

To think that one night, when my mind conjured up a dream of me looking outside my window to see a ghost no one else could see, could become a catalyst for forgiveness and acceptance, blows my ever loving mind.

I would first like to thank Represent Publishing for giving me the opportunity to share such a piece of myself through writing. It all came down to an opportunity, which, like Raina, I would initially be cautious of, but pushed myself to embrace fully and without looking back.

Next, to my partner in crime, my other (more insane & immature) half, a full fledged hug and thousand kisses thank you. Our story through the years, had it not been riddled with unwanted pain and insecurities, would never had made us who we are today. So much of what we've shared and experienced lies in these pages and I'm grateful for it. As insane as that sounds, I am grateful for it all.

And to you, lovely readers. Thank you for picking up and (hopefully) enjoying this story. I hope, if you find yourself in a dark place that you can't seem to pull yourself out of, you reach for help. There are so many people willing to help. Willing to listen. Willing to take your hand and support you.

I know you'll find your Krish. And I know you'll will find the courage to fight for your light.

About the Author

D. Allyson Howlett lives in a New England farm town with her hubbie, two boys, and three crazy house pets. She loves to practice skateboarding, is an avid fan of all things 80s, and enjoys pro-wrestling & nacho Wednesdays with her family.

She is the author of the YA series *A Playlist Kinda Love Story* and is currently working on the second novel. *Spirits n' Chai* is her second published work and first published novella.

Other novels by D. Allyson Howlett

Kisses & Stones

Wishes & Roads *coming soon!*

Thank you so much for reading! Also, check out my social media channels to learn more about my upcoming projects and releases.

Website: www.dallysonhowlett.com

Instagram: @d.allysonhowlett